Where Did My Dingo Go?

Written by Jane Clarke

Illustrated by Woody Fox

Collins

I have lost my dingo.
I looked high and low.
I cannot find my dingo.
Where did my dingo go?

Is she at the red rock?
Is she near the lake?

Did she meet a possum
or try to greet a snake?

Is she in a crystal cave?

Is she up a tree?

Is she standing on a hilltop?

Has she run away to sea?

Is she playing drums
in a band of bears?

Is she singing songs
with a tulip in her hair?

Would she ride off in a car?

Would she ride off on a train?

Did she dive into the deep?

And will I see her again?

Is she at the coral reef?

Oh, where did she go?

I asked, "Have you seen her?"
But my friends they all said no.

How I miss my pet dingo
each long day and each long night.

Oh, where did my dingo go?

And will she be all right?

She might snorkel with a shark

or hug a kangaroo!

I have lost my dingo.
So I am feeling blue.

Can you help me find my dingo?
Help me call. "Dingo!
Dingo! Can you hear me?"

19

You helped me find my dingo!
Now my life is fine.
I lost just one dingo,
but she came back with nine!

Where is
my dingo?

After reading

Letters and Sounds: Phase 5

Word count: 220

Focus phonemes: /oa/ o, ow, /oo/ ue, u, /air/ ear, /ee/ ea, /ai/ a-e, ay, ey, /igh/ i-e, i, /i/ y, /oo/ oul, /or/ al

Common exception words: oh, friend, where, of, into, the, my, she, me, said, have, so, one

Curriculum links: Geography: Locational knowledge; Science: Animals

National Curriculum learning objectives: Spoken language: listen and respond appropriately to adults and their peers; Reading/Word reading: apply phonic knowledge and skills as the route to decode words, read accurately by blending sounds in unfamiliar words containing GPCs that have been taught, read common exception words, read other words of more than one syllable that contain taught GPCs, read aloud accurately books that are consistent with their developing phonic knowledge; Reading/Comprehension: develop pleasure in reading ... by being encouraged to link what they read or hear read to their own experiences

Developing fluency

- Your child may enjoy hearing you read the story. Point to a question mark and model how to read a question.
- Now ask your child to read some of the story again, reading the questions with appropriate expression.

Phonic practice

- Ask your child to sound out each of the following words:

  b/l/ue   t/u/l/i/p

- Ask your child:
  - Can you tell me which sound is the same in each word? (/oo/)
  - Can you remember different ways to write the phoneme /oo/? Can you point to the grapheme (letter or letters) that represent the /oo/ sound in each word? (ue, u)
  - Can you think of any other words with the /oo/ sound in them? (e.g. true, huge)

Extending vocabulary

- Look at pages 22–23. Talk to your child about the animals. Ask your child if they can name any? (e.g. shark, crocodile, koala, possum, bat, emu)